Supervillain of the Day

SUPERVILLAIN OF THE DAY 2

FIRE AND ASHES

by Katie Lynn Daniels

Cover design by Jordan Miller
Interior formatting by Aubrey Hansen

Special thanks to Elizabeth Kirkwood for reading absolutely
everything I sent her, however meaningless; to Jordan Miller for his
brilliant cover designs; to Elsa for her meticulous editing; to Aubrey
Hansen for helping clueless me with formatting; to Jeremiah for his
thoughts; and to Lady Elanor for her brit picking.

Published by:
Provide Your Own – Books
PO Box 748
Tompkinsville, KY 42167
Website: Books.ProvideYourOwn.com

Print Edition, February 2013
ISBN-13: 978-0615753003 (Provide Your Own - Books)
ISBN-10: 0615753000
Library of Congress Control Number: 2013900573

To Jim and Jo
Because you gave me courage
And told me I could do anything

TABLE OF CONTENTS

PERSISTENCE

Our story begins in the fifteenth sector of the Milky Way Galaxy on a small, fast-moving planet, known primarily for the beauty of its skies. On this planet lived an alien named Floyd who became obsessed with art at a young age and grew up into a fairly unknown freelance photographer. He lived a standard yet happy life for those of his age and race, until the day his sister sold him to the Galactic Department of Supervillain Help and Relief Services for the staggering sum of ten thousand standard galactic credits. This helped her and her new husband to start their marriage off on an amazingly well-to-do foot.

The Galactic Department of Supervillain Help and Relief Services trained Floyd in standard anti-supervillain fighting techniques and sent him to an obscure planet called Earth. Earth had never heard of the Galactic Confederation, but the Galactic Politicians hoped that when they did, they would be interested in joining. Earth was due for a Supervillain outbreak at some point in the near future and it was Floyd's job to make sure that things didn't get too out of hand while the earthlings were finding their way around developing interstellar communications.

Floyd spent two years moping about and travelling and wishing he was back home again before the first supervillain made an appearance. In his very first battle, he took out twelve supervillains and a mastermind, befriended a sergeant at Scotland Yard, and suddenly realised that his life had just gotten more dangerous.

After this first battle, he discovered that there was no end to the quantity and type of supervillains that could appear in the most bizarre places, and that policemen like to ask a lot of annoying questions like:

"How was your week?"

Floyd had been on Earth long enough to know the simple things—like a week was seven days, and that five of them were business days and the remaining two were called a weekend. He hadn't been around enough people to figure out more complicated things like how his comings and goings were any business of Sergeant Joseph Adams'.

"Same as usual," he answered. "I dug a pernicious foam out of the drain system at a middle school, tracked down an army of giant killer ants by the docking ports, and tied an elastic man in knots and superglued him to make sure he couldn't get loose. I escorted at least seventeen wannabe superheroes home and lectured them about reality versus fiction, rescued a teenage girl off a crane who wasn't sure how she got there but was pretty sure it involved her boyfriend who'd turned into a monster, and assisted three cats in getting down out of trees."

"Why the cats?" Adams asked, confused.

"Because," Floyd said pointedly, "they needed me."

They'd established a routine, one that Adams stuck to religiously and Floyd never properly understood. Every Thursday, they met for lunch to exchange official and unofficial reports and news of supervillain activities. And sometimes they would talk; or Floyd would talk, and Adams would listen and ask questions. Sometimes the questions he asked were not the audible kind— they were the kind sensed rather than spoken— and those were the kinds of questions Floyd found himself answering without knowing they'd been asked; questions about life and love and home.

Adams was the only person on Earth who knew Floyd's true identity.

"So what was up with the girl on the crane then?" he asked. "Did her boyfriend turn out to be a monster?"

"No," Floyd said, annoyed. "She didn't have a boyfriend. She was an escaped patient from a mental institute. They'd been looking for her for three days, but the police didn't put much effort into it because they assumed she'd just turned into a villain."

"It does happen, you know," Adams said mildly.

"Perhaps," Floyd said vehemently, "But it's really just an excuse, and those kind of excuses can kill people. It's high time the police force recognised supervillains as a real threat and started doing something about it besides sitting back and making pathetic excuses!"

"What would you like them to do?" Adams asked, surprisingly unoffended by this outburst.

"Start by creating a special supervillain division," Floyd said. "Train officers to recognise the difference between human and superhuman activities, and how to deal with them. Investigate every crime, and not just the ones that look ordinary."

"We already have a supervillain department," Adams said confidently.

He grinned at the confusion that spread across his companion's face. "It's called Floyd."

"Oh please," Floyd said, and rolled his eyes.

"What's all that?" Adams pointed to the stack of books that the alien had carried in.

"Books," Floyd said, grinning mischievously.

"These are comic books," Adams said, stating the obvious.

"Yes," Floyd agreed. "they are."

The policeman picked up the book on the top and stared at the tightly-clad, muscular figure portrayed on the front. "It's odd," he said reflectively. "How did comic book writers so accurately predict a calamity that had never been seen before? It's almost like they were warned."

Floyd laughed. "Hardly accurate," he said. "What's the number one rule of a supervillain invasion? No superheroes," he answered his own question. "What's the main attraction of all those comic books you have there?"

Adams sighed and set the book down on top of the stack.

"There's no such thing as superheroes," he recited automatically. "It would be nice if there were though, wouldn't it?"

4

Floyd winced. "Are you that eager to get rid of me?" he asked accusingly. "Seriously, though. If superheroes did exist, and if they were anything like the ones portrayed in this stack of trash, they'd be more trouble than they were worth. Bumbling about with their emotional problems and their alter egos, endangering civilians with petty feuds, ineffective at best in getting the job done and, more often, just plain stupid. Even the villains are wildly inaccurate," he continued. "Take this one for example."

He pulled a book off the bottom of the stack, sending the top half toppling. Adams caught them before they fell to the floor. Floyd held up his choice.

"This guy transforms from an ordinary human into a huge, green, hulking monster and then back again. That violates every version of the laws of physics known to the Galactic Science Committee. Once you transform, there's no going back. You're stuck as a monster. Forever."

"That brings us to a very interesting question," Adams said, restacking the pile neatly. "What are you, of all people, doing with a stack of comic books?"

Floyd stared at the pile guiltily. "Isn't it amazing how accurately humanity could predict a calamity that has never occurred on their planet?" he tried, grinning lopsidedly.

Adams' eyes narrowed. "I think you like them," he accused. "Secretly you want to be a superhero running around earning praise and adoration..."

"A superhero?" Floyd spluttered. "Me?"

"You're right," Adams said. "You're not quite tall enough to be as imposing as a superhero should be."

"Oi!" Floyd protested, eyes flashing. Before he could continue to protest, a little man wearing glasses and carrying a clipboard bumped into him.

"Excuse me," he said, pushing his glasses up further on his nose. "Did I hear...superhero?"

"Private conversation," Floyd snapped. "Mind your own business."

"No, no, no," he said. "I'm not intruding, really. My name is Sanders." He grinned broadly, as though that explained everything.

"So?" Floyd said, blankly.

The smile vanished. "What?" Sanders asked.

"What do you want?" Floyd asked impatiently.

"Oh, yes." Sanders cleared his throat, eager to get back on script. "I work for Doctor Sinister, the most evil supervillain known in the history of supervillains—"

"Go away," Floyd cut him off.

"Excuse me?"

"Go away," Floyd repeated. "I'm having a nice conversation with my friend and you're interrupting. So scat."

Sanders looked at Adams as though seeing him for the first time. "He's a cop," he said.

"I know that," Floyd retorted. "Shoo."

"But you don't understand!" Sanders protested. "I need to have this conversation with you, now!"

"Perhaps," Floyd said. "But the thing about a conversation is that they take two people, and you're on your own."

6

"But—but," he stammered. "You're Floyd, aren't you?"

Floyd shrugged. "So?"

"So, you're a superhero! And my master, Doctor Sinister—"

"Let's get one thing straight," Floyd said angrily. "There is no such thing as superheroes. And if there were, I wouldn't be one. Goodbye."

"But Doctor Sinister is the most important supervillain in England!" Sanders argued. "And he defies you to stop his sinister plans!"

"Doctor Sinister is a joke," Floyd said. "A sideshow villain. A no one. And you can tell him I said as much. Now are you going to leave peaceably or am I going to throw you through the window?"

"But," Sanders stammered. "Doctor Sinister will be very angry with me if I—if I don't settle this..."

Floyd sighed and started to stand. Adams caught his wrist.

"Leave him alone," he said, addressing Sanders.

The little man gaped.

"You heard me," Adams repeated calmly. "You've said your piece, and he clearly doesn't want to talk to you any further. So you can leave now."

Sanders started to protest, and then abruptly shut his mouth and left.

"Now that's not fair," Floyd said, once he was out of earshot. "How come he listened to you and not me?"

Adams shrugged. "It's that special aura that comes with being a law enforcement officer," he said. "People can sense authority when I'm around."

"What about me?" Floyd complained. "I beat up bad guys every day and no one runs from me."

"It's all in the eyes," Adams said. "You're just too shifty-looking for anyone to take you seriously."

"Shifty?" Floyd repeated. "Now you're calling me shifty?"

"Actually," Adams said, looking past him. "That Sanders fellow is being shifty."

Floyd craned around to look. "I thought he was gone."

"No, he's not. He's making a call."

"That's not good," Floyd said, standing. "I don't like sneaky henchmen who go around calling their superiors when I tell them to get lost. Hey you!" he shouted in the direction of Sanders. "What do you think you're—"

He broke off abruptly, coughing on the billowing smoke that began to fill the room. It was foul-smelling and vaguely purple in colour. It piled into a column beside Sanders and solidified gradually, leaving behind a large, over-dressed villain.

"Mwahaha!" he laughed boisterously, spreading his arms wide. The other patrons of the restaurant screamed in fear or cowered behind their tables. Floyd folded his arms and waited.

The villain stopped laughing and stared at Floyd.

"Who are you?" he demanded in a deep, booming voice.

"This is the superhero, sir," Sanders said, bowing. "The one called Floyd who refused to answer your summons."

8

"I think that we should clear up a little misunderstanding," Floyd said. "I'm not a superhero."

"You're not?" Doctor Sinister said in some surprise.

"I'm not," Floyd said confidently. "Are we done here?"

"Isn't it true that you fight supervillains?" Doctor Sinister said, still confused.

"Is it true that you fight supervillains?" Floyd retorted.

"Well, on occasion," he admitted. "When they get in my way."

"Well then," Floyd said, gesturing widely. "I think we're done."

"I don't understand," Doctor Sinister said. "Are you saying you're a supervillain?"

"No," Floyd shrugged. "I'm a reporter."

"He's lying," Sanders hissed.

"No, no, that can't be," the villain said, scratching his head. "Heroes don't lie."

"There, see?" Floyd said. "Yet another reason they don't exist."

"This is all very confusing, Sanders," the villain said. "I don't see how you could have made this kind of mistake."

"It's not a mistake," Sanders continued to protest. "This person here is Floyd, known superhero vigilante."

"Ah, you used the v word," Floyd warned.

"V-word?" Sanders said, confused.

"My friend is a police officer," Floyd explained, pointing. "They don't like vigilantes all that well. You might want to scoot along now, before he notices."

"We are not vigilantes!" Doctor Sinister roared. "We are supervillains! Or, I'm a supervillain. He's a henchman. And you are a superhero!"

"Wrong," Floyd said, quite calmly. "You are a supervillain, he is a henchman, and I am a reporter."

"Maybe he's the wrong guy," Doctor Sinister suggested, in exasperation.

"Now that we've established that, can I go back to my lunch, please?" Floyd asked.

"Are you telling me that I'm wrong?" Doctor Sinister shouted, growing red in the face.

Floyd smiled. "That's exactly it," he said. "You are completely and utterly wrong."

"I'm sorry," an apologetic voice broke in. "But I'm going to have to ask you gentlemen to take your conversation elsewhere. You're disturbing the other customers."

"How dare you," Doctor Sinister said. "I will disintegrate you into dust so fine that you'll be getting into your customers' food for months."

"That's enough," Floyd said warningly. "We're taking this outside."

"Who do you think you are?" Doctor Sinister demanded.

"Out," Floyd said, pointing at the door.

"Do you presume to give me orders?"

"I do," Floyd said, a hard gleam coming to his eyes.

"You little—" Doctor Sinister started. Floyd's fist came out of nowhere, dealing a blow that sent the villain staggering backwards into his snivelling assistant.

"I told you!" Sanders said excitedly. "I told you there wasn't a mistake. This is him! The superhero you're supposed to battle!"

"I'm not a superhero," Floyd said, grabbing each one by the collar. "And I'm not going to battle you," he continued, dragging them towards the door.

He kicked the door open and tossed them both out onto the pavement.

"Oh yeah?" Doctor Sinister sneered, standing up. "What's going to stop me from reducing this entire building into rubble then?"

"Oh, I didn't say I wasn't going to *stop* you," Floyd said. "Just that it wouldn't be a *battle*."

Doctor Sinister and Sanders stumbled backwards instinctively as Floyd let the door close behind him and walked forwards threateningly.

"You did have one thing right," he said. "I do fight supervillains. But you missed the bit where they die."

"This was not part of the plan," Doctor Sinister said anxiously, hiding behind Sanders. "This wasn't supposed to happen."

"No," Sanders agreed. "It wasn't."

"You were supposed to set up a meeting!" Doctor Sinister said.

"Meeting?" Floyd spread his arms. "This looks like as opportune a time as any to me!"

"No," Doctor Sinister protested. "Tell him, Sanders!"

"The Doctor Sinister, most villainous villain ever made demands that you—"

Floyd caught up with them, and knocked Sanders aside.

"I don't take demands from villains," he said. "And you're not the most notable villains I've ever met either."

He grabbed Doctor Sinister and hit him again.

"I think," Doctor Sinister gasped, "We need a new plan."

"Here's a suggestion," Floyd said, grinning. "Go away."

"We will!" Doctor Sinister said. "I mean, we will be back!"

"Don't bother," Floyd said, laughing at them. He turned to go back to the restaurant and bumped into a spectator standing directly behind him. He looked up in annoyance.

"Going somewhere?" the stranger asked. He had bright red hair, almost orange, and wore a navy blue suit.

"None of your business," Floyd snapped, turning away. The stranger reached out and grabbed his wrist, twisting his arm behind his back.

"What do you think you're doing?" Floyd squawked.

"The question is, what do you think you're doing?" the stranger hissed, whispering in his ear. "Stop trying to play the hero."

"Who said anything about heroes?" Floyd demanded irritably. "Let go of me before someone gets hurt."

"I'm serious," the stranger repeated, tightening his grip.

"So am I," Floyd said through gritted teeth.

"You have no idea what you're getting into."

"Neither do you."

"Why don't you go back to doing whatever it is you really do and stop poking your nose where it doesn't belong?"

"Good advice," Floyd snapped. "I'm not the one attacking random strangers on the street."

"Really? What about those two villains you sent running?"

Floyd tried to shrug. "Personal matter," he explained. "Again, none of your business!"

"I think," the stranger said thoughtfully. "I think that you should make it your business to stay away from supervillains."

"And why would that be?" Floyd demanded. "Who *are* you?"

"Is there a problem here?" Adams interrupted smoothly.

The stranger diverted his attention to this new distraction.

"No, no problem," he said with a false smile.

"Then I suggest you let this man go and move along," Adams suggested, a world of threat in his even tone.

The stranger let go of Floyd reluctantly, shoving him away. Floyd caught his balance easily and turned to glare at his assailant.

"This isn't over," the stranger said, still smiling. "We'll meet again, Jeffry Lewis Floyd."

"He knew my name," Floyd whispered, as the stranger walked off smugly.

"Who was that?" Adams asked, staring after him.

"That?" Floyd repressed a shudder. "That was the *real* 'most evil' supervillain in London."

INTEGRITY

Mr. Stephen Hendrick was the editor of an insignificant tabloid paper called "The London Star" that usually specialised in stories of the paranormal and supernatural sort. Important news of the past included the invention of the first interstellar drive and the kidnapping of an extremely well known beauty star by malevolent aliens who used her body to send back a message of their evil intentions to all humans everywhere.

The aliens had yet to appear and the inventor of the interstellar drive had taken his invention and disappeared, but it was the news that mattered, not the follow-up.

The paper had done pretty well back in the ordinary days, where a corrupt politician or an armed robbery was the most excitement offered to the general public. An alien invasion or demonic sighting was so much more interesting and incredible. But now supervillains walked in the streets and people saw them with their own eyes. They didn't have to read about monsters made of goo or abductions by flying monkeys because they witnessed such things for themselves every day. And "The London Star" was dying as a result.

"This is abominable!" Mr. Hendrick was shouting at the top of his lungs. "Does anyone here realise that every story we have to print tonight is about the exact same subject? What sort of horrid lack of imagination has overtaken my reporters? Where are the daring men and women who used to be *different* from the rest of London; unafraid of using the brains God gave them?"

There was no answer, of course. The rest of the staff bustled about getting ready to print a paper consisting entirely of reports of supervillain attacks. Regardless of whether or not the Editor approved, that was all the material they had.

In the midst of all this chaos Floyd appeared like the god of mischief himself.

"Good morning," he said airily.

"Jeffry Floyd," said the clerk at the desk, smiling smugly. Floyd paused, poised for flight.

"What's wrong?" he asked warily.

"Nothing," she said, still smiling. "You're just late."

"No later than usual," he said, checking the clock over the door to be sure.

"Then what are you worried about?" she asked.

"You're smiling," Floyd said. "You never smile at me. Unless you just did something I'm really, really not going to look forward to."

"The Editor is in a temper," she offered, trying to hide her grin.

"Uh, tell me something I don't know?"

"You're a moron?" she suggested.

"Again," Floyd repeated. "Something I already knew."

"The Editor wants to see you," she said formally.

"See?" Floyd said, gesturing. "Something new! Finally. Was it really that hard?"

He started to walk past her into the inner sanctum but froze when he heard her next sentence.

"He said you're his last hope."

Slowly Floyd turned around to stare.

"What did you say?" he asked, genuinely unsure.

"You're his last hope," Mary Margaret repeated. "So I suggest you be on your best behaviour."

"Last hope," Floyd repeated slowly. "What exactly does that mean?"

Mary Margaret picked up her pen and pretended to be busy.

"What do you mean?" Floyd repeated. "Come on, help me out here!"

She continued to ignore him.

"Floyd!" a voice bellowed from behind him. Slowly Floyd turned to see Mr. Hendrick standing in the doorway.

"In my office," the Editor snapped. "Now."

Meekly, Floyd followed.

"You're late," the editor said without preamble, leaving Floyd to shut the door. He plopped down in his oversized rolling desk chair. "You were supposed to be here at nine this morning."

"I'm always late," Floyd pointed out. "You don't usually take a personal interest."

"Show me what you've got," the editor demanded.

Cautiously, Floyd set his books on the desk and reached into his coat pocket for the article he'd printed out that morning.

"What are these?" the editor asked in interest, pulling the pile over.

"Those are mine," Floyd said hastily.

"They're comic books," Mr. Hendrick observed.

"Thank you for enlightening me on that point," Floyd said, making no attempt to hide his sarcasm.

"You know, these people had the right idea," the Editor said thoughtfully. "Caped crusaders flying around, saving the helpless and innocent, that's real heroism and romance. Wouldn't you say?"

"Romance?" Floyd snorted in derision. "It's ridiculous."

"But it's what people want," Mr. Hendrick said firmly. "They need the reassurance in this time of crisis."

"Crisis?" Floyd repeated again. "When did you get to be so sappy?"

"Since every single one of my reporters started writing about the same thing!" Mr. Hendrick yelled. "All anyone ever hears about any more is supervillains this, supervillains that! Even the Times is reporting about supervillains and do you know what? No one cares any more!"

Floyd listened to this rant with mild interest.

"We need to give them something different," Mr. Hendrick finished, slapping the desk for emphasis. "We need to give them hope for the future. *You* need to give them hope, Floyd."

Floyd started. "Me?" he said, struggling to catch up. "What am I supposed to do?"

"Report on superhero sightings around the city," the Editor said eagerly. "That's the story that will renew interest in this paper.

"Put that away," he said, gesturing the pages Floyd held folded in his hand. "I'll pay you double for this job, if you do a good job for me."

"You want me to write about superheroes?" Floyd repeated, dumbfounded.

"Not just write about it," the Editor said, caught up in his own idea. "I want you to do your research carefully. Make people really believe in it."

"You want me to write a story about superheroes," Floyd said.

"Would you stop repeating that like a parrot?" Mr. Hendrick said impatiently. "Yes, I want you to write a story about superheroes! Show some enthusiasm."

"But I don't want to," Floyd blurted out.

"You read this trash," Mr. Hendrick said, tossing the comic books at him. "Why wouldn't you want to write it?"

"Because," he faltered. "Because they don't exist."

"And when was the last time you reported about something that did exist?"

Floyd opened his mouth and shut it again.

"Why don't you ask someone else?" he blurted out. "Anyone would jump at the chance to get double pay."

"Except you," the Editor growled. "This is your line of work. Now stop griping and get to it!"

"No," Floyd said abruptly.

"What?"

"No," Floyd repeated. "I won't do it."

The Editor blinked as though he wasn't quite sure what to make of that.

"Why ever not?" he demanded.

"Because superheroes don't exist," Floyd said stubbornly.

"So?" the Editor demanded. "Since when has that been a problem for you?"

"This is different," Floyd said.

"Different how?"

Floyd started to answer, and changed his mind. What was he going to say? That inventing danger was somehow different from offering false hope?

"I won't do it," he said instead, shaking his head defiantly. "I won't do your dirty work for you."

"Floyd," the Editor sighed, torn between outrage and condescension. "I hired you to do my dirty work for me. That's your job."

"Not this time," he said with conviction.

"You write me a superhero story," Mr. Hendrick threatened, "Or I'll... I'll..."

"You'll what?" Floyd taunted, gathering his things.

"I'll fire you!" Mr. Hendrick shouted at his retreating back. "Come back with that superhero story or don't come back at all."

Floyd let the door slam shut behind him and didn't look back.

MERCY

Floyd couldn't stop thinking about heroes.

Heroes don't exist, he told himself. They never had, and they never would. People are selfish creatures, unwilling to sacrifice for others. This is a universal law of the universe. Once he had believed in heroes. That was before he woke up in a white prison cell and realised he'd been betrayed by one.

Heroes were a fairytale, ranking right up there with freedom and the fountain of youth.

And yet... and yet...

So many people believed in heroes. So many people walked through their entire life thinking that there were those who chose to sacrifice—to risk their own lives to save others.

And to what end? When had believing in anything made the slightest difference in life?

Floyd smiled bitterly at the answer. It hadn't.

It was all stupid. People were stupid, believing was stupid, and heroes were stupid. Could something that didn't exist be stupid?

Floyd peered at the sky for the answer, and that's when he saw the smoke.

The smoke was black and billowing just enough to be noticeable. The fire was either far away or too small to be of serious concern. Still, Floyd didn't have anything else to do so he started walking in that direction.

The narrow street was blocked almost entirely by fire engines. Floyd was surprised to see the building was a church, and noticed the well-dressed people standing around talking, pointing, and looking generally horrified and dishevelled. Black ash smeared their faces and previously spotless clothing. There was blood and tears and ambulances.

Sobered by the sight, Floyd approached a man in a suit who didn't appear to be otherwise occupied.

"What happened here?" he asked.

"There was a fire," the man said simply, looking down on him in surprise.

"That's unusual, isn't it?" Floyd pressed. "How often do fires start during a service?"

"Never," the man said. "There's no way it could have started. We have safeguards in place for such things. Sprinkler systems and... and the church is made of brick. It shouldn't have burned."

"But it did?" Floyd said. "How did the fire start, then?"

"I don't know," the man mumbled. "I can't talk to you any more."

Floyd watched him as he walked away, intuitively knowing that there was more to the story.

"Excuse me," he said to an elderly lady, who had only a fine layer of ash dusting her outfit. "Do you know how the fire started? Did you see anything unusual?"

"I'll tell you what happened, young man," she said in a high-pitched quavering voice, poking him with her cane. "A fiend from hell started that fire. That's what happened."

"Did you see him?" Floyd asked.

"Yes, I did," she said confidently. "He stood up in the middle of the service and then he burst into flames."

"Wait," Floyd put a hand on her arm as she started to walk away. "He burst into flames himself?"

"That's what I said," the old lady repeated. "Do you want me to say it again?"

Floyd let her go and kept walking through the crowd. Once he left the ring of fire engines and approached the building, he found his way blocked by yellow crime scene tape and determined law enforcement officers left to guard the premises.

"So what's going on here?" Floyd asked conversationally, careful to keep to his side of the tape.

"Move along now," the constable he addressed said.

"I am moving," Floyd retorted. "Why is a church a crime scene?"

"It's a suspected arson case," the constable said warily.

"Arson?" Floyd said, pretending to exhibit surprise. "Any ideas who did it?"

The constable glanced over his shoulder, eager to gossip but worried about his superiors.

"They say he died in the flames," he confided. "Burned to a crisp. But they're having trouble identifying the bodies."

Floyd took a step backwards, all the banter suddenly gone out of his face. "Bodies?" he repeated.

"Quite a few of them," the constable said cheerfully. "They say it's unusual to have this high a death count in a fire."

"How high?" Floyd asked softly.

The constable shrugged. "I heard ten, fifteen maybe," he said.

Floyd felt suddenly like he was going to be sick. "I have to go," he whispered, and ran from the scene.

The road was crowded and he wove in and out of emergency vehicles and personnel, ignoring the shouts of people he cut in front of, just trying to get away from the smoke and the death.

And then he ran headlong into someone, someone who grabbed him by the arms and didn't let go. Floyd looked up into the startling blue eyes of the redheaded stranger.

"You need to start watching where you're going," the stranger said. "You could hurt someone."

Floyd didn't have the patience for a game of banter and wit. He brought his knee up into the taller man's groin and used the momentum to tumble backwards and wrest himself out of his opponents grip. Then he ran again.

"What are you in such a hurry for?" the stranger called after him. "Don't you want to know who's responsible for all these fires?"

Floyd froze, and turned slowly. "What fires?" he asked.

The stranger laughed. "Don't you know?" he said. "There's an arsonist in town. And he's getting quite a reputation. He's also impossible to catch."

Floyd took a step back. "You're responsible," he said, trembling with anger instead of fear. "You killed all those people."

"It's what supervillains do," the stranger said, laughing.

Floyd took a moment to actually look at him. He was wearing blue jeans and a formerly white t-shirt. Both were torn and burned and he was covered in ashes. But there was a gleam in his eye of maniacal joy and excitement, thrill and mesmerising power.

"Tell me your name," Floyd hissed, taking another step towards him.

The stranger laughed at him. "You're a child," he taunted. "A pretender. Go home and stop sticking your nose where it doesn't belong."

"Give me a name!" Floyd screamed.

"I'll give you a name," the stranger said agreeably. "But only so that you can make sure you avoid me."

Floyd waited.

"You can call me Ashes," the villain said. Floyd didn't wait around for more.

....

"Excuse me, sir," said the clerk at Scotland Yard. "Can I help you?"

"Sergeant Adams," Floyd said without preamble. "Where is he?"

"I believe he's in the lounge," the clerk said. "But you can't go back there without a visitors pass. Do you—"

He broke off and resorted to shouting as Floyd pushed past him and ran into the depths of the building.

"Adams!" he shouted, sliding to a halt in the doorway. "I need everything you know about dead people. And fires. Fires involving dead people in, say, the last two weeks."

"Who is this?" an inspector asked, looking up in disdain.

"I'll handle this," Adams said, standing quickly. He clamped a hand on Floyd's collar and marched him out.

"Please," Floyd added, as though that would help.

"You can't just come barging in here demanding information," Adams said firmly.

"There was a fire in a church," Floyd said abruptly.

"Yes, I know," Adams said. "We're having trouble with an arsonist."

"People died," Floyd pleaded. "I need to know how many people."

"Floyd," Adams repeated firmly.

"I need to know about the other fires," Floyd continued, rushing ahead. "I need to know why you think they're connected. I need a death count, Joseph."

"The fire station would have better information for you," Adams said.

"I know you have the records here," Floyd argued. "If it's an arsonist then Scotland Yard will be involved. And you're looking to charge him with homicide as well."

"That's correct. It's still none of your business."

"Yes, it is," Floyd said, pulling away and standing his ground. "Because I met your mass murderer. And I know his name."

"Well tell me!" Adams exclaimed.

"Ashes," Floyd said simply.

"So it's a supervillain?" Adams clarified.

"Of course it's a supervillain," Floyd sighed. "Would I be here otherwise?"

"Obviously not," Adams said sarcastically. "Do you even have a plan, Floyd?"

"Find it and kill it," Floyd said bitterly.

"That's not much of a plan."

"It's all I've got. Are you going to help or not?"

"Call me in the morning," Adams said, showing him the door.

"What?" Floyd said in disbelief.

"Call me in the morning," Adams repeated, and shut the door behind him.

1HONOUR

Floyd woke up to someone shouting his name. He put a pillow over his head and tried to ignore it, but then the someone resorted to shaking him and he gave up in despair.

"Leave me alone," he started to say, but it didn't come out in English and he broke off in confusion.

The flat was dim with early morning light and the face of Sergeant Adams peered down at him anxiously. He was in full uniform, his helmet held securely under his left arm.

"What?" Floyd said in annoyance, double checking his language. "How did you get in?"

"You have to come with me," Adams said. "Now. You have five minutes to get dressed."

"Why?" Floyd asked, still tired and grumpy. "What are you doing here? Did you break in?"

"No," Adams said, a tinge of impatience marring his cool professional exterior. "I made copies of your keys last month."

"Is that legal?" Floyd demanded.

"You're an illegal alien," Adams said. "You don't have any rights. Now get dressed and come with me."

"Why?" Floyd repeated for the third time.

Adams sighed and gave up. "There's been another fire," he said.

"So?"

"It's still burning," Adams said. "I think you should get over there as quickly as possible if you want to work out what kind of villain this is."

Floyd stopped arguing and got dressed, following Adams out of the flat without protest. They drove twenty minutes without conversation, tense with the seriousness of the situation. But when the police car came to a halt and they looked around there were no flames to be seen. Hardly any smoke rose from the charred ruins that lay like a giant's scattered playthings.

Floyd's face paled at the devastation and his breathing quickened, but Adams didn't notice, hastening towards the sound of arguing coming from one of the fire engines.

"I've got people in there dying, and you're worried that we're destroying evidence? I don't care about your evidence. You stay out of my way until I'm sure that everyone is saved who can be saved. Are we clear?"

The first voice was deep and authoritative, tinged with exhaustion and desperation.

"If you don't let me get some detectives in there this arsonist could start another fire and more people could die," a second voice said argumentatively. "Is that what you want? You want more deaths on your head?"

"My job is to save lives."

"And my job is to stop the bad guys. So why don't you stop getting in my way?"

Adams paused within sight of a fire chief and the detective inspector from Scotland Yard, vehemently arguing.

"I told you why I can't stop getting in the way." The fireman sounded weary. He was dirty and hot and looked like he needed sleep.

"I'm telling you to step aside and let my men in there," the inspector said impatiently. He was dressed in a tan suit and though his face was turning red from the effort of shouting he looked as crisp as a Monday morning.

Floyd looked out over the wreckage. Twisted metal and piles of concrete obscured the interior of the factory, but he could hear the shouts of the firemen who risked their lives to see if anyone was still alive. Somehow he knew they wouldn't find any survivors. He closed his eyes and counted to ten. When he opened them again the nightmare was still there.

"I don't care what protocol says," the fire chief was saying. "As long as there is any possibility that there are people in there we're going to do our best to save them."

"And every moment that you delay the person responsible for this is getting farther away!" the inspector retorted.

"Go in there if you want," the fire chief said. "Do your job. But if you'd been doing it properly in the first place this would never have happened."

"I want you to get your people out of there before they destroy the evidence," the inspector argued.

"What evidence?" the fire chief asked. "The place was burned to the ground!"

"And who's fault was that?" the inspector asked. "What sort of code violations were they getting away with in there that you were supposed to be inspecting?"

"Don't talk to me about code violations when you should have caught this guy last week!"

"Do you know how hard it is to catch a criminal when you have to wait hours to get your hands on the evidence?"

"Enough!"

Floyd's scream cut through the argument and they turned to him in surprise. His face was wet with tears when he turned from the wreckage to the authorities.

"There's no point," he said vehemently. "They're all dead. Don't you get that? They're all dead!"

"How do you know?" the fire chief asked.

"Who is this guy?" the detective inspector demanded.

"He's done leaving survivors," Floyd said. "He's trying to frighten us. Make us panic. And it's working. When we're so swept up in the hows and the whys we forget the tragedy that's taken place and that's when he'll burn again and again..."

"How do you know this?" the fire chief said, agitated. "Do you know who is responsible?

Floyd shook off the question. "They were people," he said, staring at the factory again. "They had lives and children and husbands and sweethearts. They worked and played and fought and drank and now they're gone and there's nothing left and why? So that one maniac can prove he's better than me?"

"This isn't about you," Adams repeated uneasily.

"Who are you?" the inspector said, advancing threateningly.

The fire chief stopped him. "Can you help us?" he asked Floyd.

Floyd put his face in his hands.

"Get a grip, Floyd," Adams suggested. "We need your help here."

"Sergeant," the inspector snapped. "Do you know this man?"

"He said he had information that would help us," Adams replied.

"There are lives yet to be saved," the fire chief said, folding his arms. "Anything you tell us could be of use."

"Supervillains?" Floyd said, raising his eyebrows.

The fire chief shrugged. "They exist," he said. "So hit me with it."

Floyd took a deep breath and launched into his analysis. "It can't be arson," he said. "There is no chemical compatible with Earth's physics that allows this kind of fire to result. We know that Earth is under quarantine, so it didn't come from another planet. So it can't be a mastermind, or a genius or anything like that."

"Quarantine?" the inspector said. "What are you talking about?"

"Go on," the fire chief instructed.

"That leaves superpowers," Adams prompted.

"That leaves superpowers," Floyd agreed. "There are only two kind of superpowers involving fire. Three, actually. One: you shoot fire out of your fingertips, or other bodily orifices. Two: becoming a rampaging fire breathing monster. Three: a human torch.

"If it were a rampaging fire-breathing monster I think there would be reports of a rampaging fire-breathing monster. It's the kind of thing that's rather hard to miss. But no one has reported seeing anything like that; just the fire that comes and goes and burns and leaves nothing behind it..."

He glanced back at the factory, and froze.

"Don't look at that," Adams said, taking his arm and forcing him to look the other way. "Go on."

Floyd stared into the distance, collecting his thoughts.

"The time delay is an interesting aspect," he said thoughtfully. "Why the delay? Why not go instantly from place to place lighting everything on fire?"

"It could be telling us something about his motives," the fire chief said. "Why he's targeting these specific areas, how long it takes him to prepare, and so forth."

"Or it tells us about his strengths and weaknesses," Floyd responded. "If he could just shoot fire at a building and have it burst into flame then he would. Since he's not doing that it probably means he can't. He has to be there the whole time, and he has to regenerate afterwards."

"So that leaves a human torch?" Adams asked.

"You're catching on fast," Floyd said.

"What are we talking about now?" the inspector sneered. "Fairytales?"

"So we're dealing with a human torch," Adam said, ignoring him. "How do we defeat it?"

"I don't know," Floyd said helplessly. "Fire is extremely rare as a superpower. I think there's been maybe two, three human torches on record. I don't think anyone ever defeated them."

"Water won't put out the flames," the fire chief offered.

"It's fuelled by the pure energy of the villain's life force," Floyd explained. "Until that runs out he's invulnerable."

"Is there some way to keep him from burning?" the fire chief asked. "We've got to stop him somehow, right? So maybe if we can find him we can lock him up or something."

"I don't know," Floyd said, pulling on his hair in distraction. "I don't know. There's so little data. Nothing to pull from. I'll—I'll have to ask him."

"What?" Adams said, shocked.

"Do you know where to find him?" the fire chief asked.

"He's taunting me," Floyd said. "I think, if I let him, that he'll find me."

"Are you sure you want that?" Adams asked worriedly.

"Maybe I can kill him in human form," Floyd said. "I don't know. I have to try, right? I have to try something..."

"It could be very dangerous to approach him," the fire chief cautioned. "You shouldn't take unnecessary risk."

Floyd laughed semi-hysterically.

"Calm down," Adams said warningly. "You said you met him before. Do you have a name?"

"Remember the red-haired stranger from the day before yesterday?" Floyd asked.

"Yeah," Adams said, vaguely uneasy.

"That was him," Floyd said. "I saw him at the church fire yesterday. His name is Ashes."

"And he said he was responsible?" the fire chief asked.

Floyd swallowed and nodded.

"We have a name," Adams said. "That's a start. How do we find him?"

Floyd shrugged. "Follow the fire," he suggested. "I guess he has to renew his strength at intervals, which is why he stops burning. But he's getting stronger. He's moving up."

"So his next target will be something bigger?" the fire chief clarified. "That doesn't narrow the field much."

"I'm sorry," Floyd said. "That's all I know. And that it will take him roughly 24 hours before he burns again."

"Which doesn't give us much time," the fire chief said grimly.

"That's what I've been telling you," the inspector broke in, grateful to turn the conversation back to mediocre subjects. "We've got to get in there and track this guy before he disappears for good."

He glared at the group, but no one answered.

"Don't you have some place to be, Sergeant?" he snapped in annoyance.

"Yes sir," Adams said, coming sharply to attention. "Come on, Floyd."

He took Floyd's elbow and started to lead him back to the police car when they were interrupted by raucous evil laughter sprouting behind them. Floyd turned around in disbelief.

"Do you see all this?" Doctor Sinister asked, spreading his arms in a grand gesture towards the burned out factory. "All this ruin, all this devastation—it is mine!"

Floyd folded his arms and sighed.

"This is the arsonist?" the fire chief asked in disbelief.

"No, this is an idiot," Floyd said.

"And where is that fool, that coward, who will fail to save this world from utter destruction?" Doctor Sinister continued pompously. "Where is the hero who calls himself Floyd?"

"Over here," Floyd said, waving. "What do you think you're doing?"

"You will meet my challenge," Doctor Sinister said in his most sinister voice. "Or I will continue to wreak destruction and havoc on this city!"

"Right," Floyd said sarcastically. "And we're all so afraid of your toy ray guns and smoky transporter. I see you left your bumbling clerk at home this time—is he doing your laundry for you too? Now get out of here before I decide to kill just to put you out of your unimpressive misery."

"Unimpressive?" Doctor Sinister bristled. "What do you mean, I'm unimpressive?" he shouted. "I'm the most impressive supervillain ever! *You're* the one with an alter ego as a reporter! Talk about a worn out trope."

"It's not my alter ego," Floyd said patiently. "It's my real world job. And you're the one wearing mismatched socks in public."

Doctor Sinister looked down at his feet. One sock was blue and one was red.

"I always wear my socks that way," he said.

"Of course you do," Floyd agreed. He didn't mean it, and Doctor Sinister knew he didn't mean it and Floyd knew Doctor Sinister knew he didn't mean it, and so they stared at each other making sure they both knew what the other one knew.

"How dare you," Doctor Sinister roared. "We're going to settle this here and now."

"Do you know how many people died here today?" Floyd asked tersely. "Neither do we. But it was more people than you can ever hope to hurt given an entire lifetime of crime. Does that mean anything to you? It means that you are not my biggest problem. In fact, you don't even make it onto my list of problems worth dealing with. So why don't you shut up and go away before more people die from your stupidity?"

"I do not do your bidding, human!"

"Stop calling me human," Floyd snapped. "It's insulting. Let's go, Joseph."

"This isn't over," Doctor Sinister kept shouting. "I will hunt you down and kill you like the coward you are. I will make your life miserable until you crawl back to me begging for the mercy I once showed you."

"Are you really a superhero?" the fire chief asked curiously.

"No," Floyd sighed. "I really am just a reporter who knows far more about supervillains than is healthy."

"I will see you disgraced and humiliated," Doctor Sinister continued. "I will see you eat the dirt at my feet and humbly beg my forgiveness! I will see you swear your undying obedience to my will and then, and then! Then I will turn you away and reject your most abject loyalty."

"What do we do about him?" the fire chief asked anxiously. "He seems like he means business."

"Oh, don't worry about him," Floyd said carelessly. "He'll disappear in a puff of smoke as soon as I'm out of sight."

"Literally?" the fire chief asked dubiously.

Floyd grinned. "Literally," he promised.

"This isn't over yet Floyd of the... Floyd the... The most..." The villain stumbled over the title that Floyd didn't have. "This isn't over yet—"

Floyd slammed the car door, and drove out of sight.

Doctor Sinister vanished in a puff of smoke.

RESPONSIBILITY 5

"Where are you taking me?" Floyd asked, staring out the window listlessly.

"Home," Adams said. "And then I'm going to work. You have a job—you could go to work too."

"Mmm," Floyd said. "I don't think I have a job any more."

"Why is that?"

"I disagreed with the editor."

"Over..." Adams prompted.

"He wanted me to write about superheroes," Floyd explained.

"So? Write about superheroes."

"They don't exist."

Adams snorted in derision. "Neither do alien abductions," he retorted.

"Oi!" Floyd protested. "Abducted alien speaking here."

"Whatever," Adams said. "The point remains that you're already notoriously unreliable as a news source. So what's the issue?"

Floyd squirmed. "I just don't like lying to people," he confessed.

Again, the policeman laughed. "Where did this sudden onslaught of morality come from?" he asked.

Floyd didn't answer, but Adams looked at him expectantly.

"You want to know what my problem with it is?" he exploded. "All I ever hear from anyone any more is heroes this, and heroes that. Floyd, come be a hero and rescue us. Tell us what you know, Floyd, so that we can save the world. Even the villains are all 'Oh, Floyd, the great superhero, come defeat us.' And now I'm supposed to *write* about superheroes to give hope to people that things will get better! But the fact of the matter is that they're not. Things are never going to get better. In fact, they're probably going to get worse! And there's nothing anyone can do about it and there aren't going to be any heroes coming to the rescue. Do you know why there's no such thing as heroes? Because this isn't a comic book. This isn't a film. This is the real world! And when people are heroes in the real world *they die*."

Adams raised his eyebrows but didn't say anything. After glaring at him for a moment Floyd went back to staring moodily out the window.

"Are you done?" Adams asked finally.

"Yeah," Floyd said shortly.

"Good," Adams said. "Because this is your stop."

Floyd sighed and opened the door. "Call me if anything happens," he muttered.

....

For several hours Floyd sat still and tried to write about government conspiracies and superhero cover-ups and strange unexplained sightings of caped crusaders around the city. But every attempt ended up in a crumpled ball on the floor. Finally he gave up on writing anything on the paper at all, just taking one sheet at a time, slowly crumpling it, and throwing it at the wall. Gradually it dawned on him that he was waiting for the phone to ring.

He picked up the phone and dialed Scotland Yard.

"Any developments?" he asked, once he had Adams on the line.

Adams sighed. "You're sitting at home waiting for the phone to ring, aren't you?" he asked.

"What?" Floyd said, feigning incredulity. "No. Of course not. I just thought I'd... check in," he finished lamely, and sighed. "Of course I'm sitting at home waiting for the phone to ring," he said. "What else am I supposed to do?"

"Go out and do something," Adams suggested. "Go chase down shadows or villains or something. Whatever it is you usually do when you're not hanging around like a needy puppy dog."

"I do not hang around like a—" Floyd started to protest indignantly and broke off, realising the futility of it.

"Go kill something," Adams suggested.

"What if I'm out when you call?" Floyd asked anxiously. "What if I can't get there in time because I'm distracted by... whatever I find to distract me?"

"Many years ago humankind invented something called a cell phone," Adams said patiently. "Get one."

43

"I could do that," Floyd said. "And do you know how long I'd have one? Until the next supervillain throws me against a wall."

"Suit yourself," Adams said wearily. "Just find something to keep yourself busy."

Floyd sighed. "Call me if anything happens," he repeated, and hung up.

He stared moodily at the crumpled paper on the floor for a few minutes before losing patience and going out.

....

It was two hours before dawn, but Floyd had no way of knowing that from where he sat, sprawled in the corner of a holding cell. They'd locked him up around midnight, and he'd been glad to see them go, but satisfied that they were eager to get away from him. Humans were so fun to torment verbally.

As much as he tried to pretend his head wasn't being split open by a cricket bat, he couldn't outthink the pain, so he consoled himself by talking out loud. The other drunken and irritated occupants of the cell tried to ignore him, but Floyd could be singularly hard to ignore when he put his mind to it. So then they tried to forcibly shut him up, but Floyd was used to fighting supervillains and had no issue with a bunch of average humans in an enclosed space.

He was interrupted in this violent diversion by the rapid approach of policemen, and not just any policemen either.

"Joseph?"

He gave a half-hearted lop-sided grin in response to Adams' grim stare.

"Get him out of there," Adams said in resignation. "Pull yourself together, Floyd. We've got a situation."

"Hey," Floyd shrugged. "You told me to go kill something. The something just happened to disagree in an unlawful manner."

"You're drunk," Adams stated.

"Yeah," Floyd agreed. "That happens to me sometimes. Have I mentioned how much I hate this planet?"

He was pulled out of the cell by a guard, who closed and locked the door behind him. Adams looked down at him in disgust for a moment, and then slapped him hard across the face.

"Ow," Floyd protested, touching his cheek. "What was that for?"

"Follow me," Adams ordered, walking away. Floyd followed, still complaining.

"You can't blame me," he muttered. "I was sitting at home minding my own business, waiting for the phone to ring, and pestering you. You're the one who told me to get out and do something. I was just doing what you said. It's all your fault."

"Shut up," Adams ordered.

The fog outside the police station was grey with the pale light of morning. It was thick as pea soup, and dampened what little sound there was at this hour. Floyd blinked, and soaked in the sombre, subdued atmosphere. Adams shoved him into the back of a police car and shut the door, and suddenly clarity hit him like a beam of sunlight.

Floyd swore.

"Was that an 'I've been such an idiot' sort of oath or an 'I'm still being an idiot' one?" Adams asked caustically.

"The former," Floyd said. "Although I still hold that I'd be sitting in my flat being miserable right now if it weren't for you."

"I just gave the advice," Adams said. "You're responsible for what you did with it."

"What happened?" Floyd begged. "Are we too late? Can I do anything? How many—"

He broke off.

"We're on our way," Adams said. "It's a large tenement house. Last I heard the fire was out of control, so I sincerely doubt we'll be too late."

"He's getting stronger," Floyd muttered. "Have you made any progress in finding a way to douse the flames?"

"None," Adams said. "They've resorted to fire blocks and careful monitoring to prevent spreading."

He glanced back at Floyd. "Will that work?" he asked. "Can they contain it?"

"I don't know," Floyd said. "I hope so. But I really don't know."

"Are you all right?" Adams asked.

"No," Floyd snapped. "Shut up and don't ask me again."

The scene of the fire was chaotic with people shouting orders and calling for help, running back and forth, reporters pestering firemen, and police trying to keep spectators at bay. Someone shouted for Adams and he glanced between his superior and Floyd.

"That way," he said, pointing to the tent set up for emergency management. "Go make yourself useful. Don't get into trouble."

Floyd rolled his eyes and sauntered in the direction of the tent.

"Oh not another civilian," said an irritatingly cultured voice. "Someone get him out of here?"

"Hey!" Floyd protested, looking for the speaker. "Not a civilian! Well, I am, but that's not the point. I can help."

"Wait," a familiar voice interjected. "It's okay. I know him."

"Thank goodness," Floyd said gratefully. "I don't think we were properly introduced yesterday, but I'm very glad to see you again."

"Frank Riley," the fire chief said, extending his hand. "This is Mr. Tennyson, the owner of the building."

Floyd looked around and identified Mr. Tennyson as the owner of the annoying voice. He was a slightly balding, extremely tidy middle-aged man in a suit that clearly identified him as a wealthy member of the not-working class.

"Jeffry Floyd," Floyd introduced himself. "What exactly is going on here?"

"Who is this guy?" the owner asked, annoyed.

"This is Mr. Floyd," Fire Chief Riley said. "He's helping us with this case."

"Helping how?" Tennyson sneered. "He looks like jail scum to me."

"Please," Floyd said. "Just tell me what's going on."

Riley sighed and glanced at the fire. "It's out of control," he said. "We can't make any progress in putting it out. We can't get men in there to rescue the victims."

"Victims?" Floyd said tightly.

"Very few people got out of the building when the fire started," Riley explained. "We haven't even been able to tell where it originated. You said supervillains, right? Because no ordinary fire should be able to burn like this."

"You have people trapped inside?" Floyd repeated. "How many?"

"It's hard to say," the suit said stiffly. "Far more than we'd like to add to a casualty list."

"I have to go," Floyd said desperately. "I have to stop him."

"Hold up," Riley said, catching his shoulder. "How are you going to do that?"

"I'll think of something," Floyd said, wrenching away. "I have to try."

"Try what? What are you going to do?"

"I'm going to try reason," Floyd said. "And if that doesn't work I'll start hitting things. Now listen. The minute you see that fire die you get your people in there and you rescue as many as you can. I'll try to stall as long as I can."

"Are you sure about this?" the fire chief asked.

"As sure as I can be," Floyd said earnestly. "Trust me."

"Hey listen kid," the owner said. "Anything you do is going to result in you getting killed. Stop trying to be a hero."

"I'm not a kid," Floyd snarled in reply. "And I'm not a hero."

He stalked down the road towards the flaming building just as Adams came into the tent, breathlessly.

"Where is he?" he asked. "Where did he go?"

Riley pointed in disbelief. "He's walking into the fire," he said. "He thinks he can do something."

Adams clenched his hands behind his back and watched.

COURAGE

The fire roared with heat and hunger. Flames leapt out of doors and windows, consuming, burning; reaching for the sky. Floyd walked steadily closer to the blaze, ignoring how quickly his skin dried in the heat, ignoring the wind the flames generated; ignoring all the warning signs that he should turn around and run very fast in the other direction. When the heat became too searing to watch he closed his eyes and pressed on blindly: one step at a time. One foot before the other.

When it became too hot to breathe he held his breath and kept walking. The pressure built against his chest and he felt himself falter. He stumbled, and instinctively gasped for air, only to discover that the searing heat had been replaced by burning smoke. He choked, and fell to his knees. Gathering his last breath he screamed in desperation, hurling his defiance into the blaze.

"Ashes!" he shouted, and coughed on the smoke, and waited.

The fire snuffed out as though it hadn't been. The heat receded like a wave. The roaring died away to nothing. Floyd stood and pressed on into the building.

Blackened walls and charred carpet surrounded him. He could hear the groaning of the structure, weakened by the blaze. He imagined he could hear the screams of frightened children, trapped within suffocating spaces, of people dying in pain and fear. Abandoning caution he ran.

He ran down hallways and up flights of stairs, kicking open doors at random, going from floor to floor searching, shouting. He ran blindly, without reason or purpose until Ashes reached out from behind some dark corner he'd passed without a glance, spinning him around and sending him flying backwards to slam against the wall.

His hair stood up straight, as red as Floyd remembered it. He was wearing blue jeans and a t-shirt, both torn and dirty. His face was streaked with dirt and sweat but there was a gleam in his eyes of thrill and amazement. He glowed with pure joy.

"Do you have a death wish?" he asked Floyd, laughing. "Or do you envy my power?"

"You know who I am," Floyd warned, standing slowly.

"You're the newest superhero wannabe," Ashes said with a shrug.

"No," Floyd said. "You know who I am or you wouldn't have let me in."

"And who are you, exactly?"

"I'm the person who's going to stop you," Floyd said, stepping forward. "You're not going to hurt anyone else, Ashes."

"That's right," Ashes said. "I'm not going to hurt anyone. I'm going to free them. I am the liberator of the world. I will free you all from these useless bodies and force you to burn with me."

"Who are you?" Floyd demanded.

"You're pathetic," Ashes taunted, ignoring the question. "You think you can win this game, but you don't even know the rules."

"Tell me your name," Floyd said tersely. "Your real name."

Ashes shrugged. "Sam Wainwright is who I used to be," he said. "But that's not my name any more."

"Yeah, somehow I got that," Floyd said. "So tell me about this supervillain thing. How is it working out for you?"

"Is this how you play?" Ashes asked. "With words and idle threats and taunts?"

"Sure," Floyd said. "If it will keep you distracted for a while. What about this human torch thing? Are you fire in human form? Or is a transitional power? Those are rare, you know. Transitional powers. Almost as rare as fire itself. You're quite an anomaly you know."

Ashes smiled. "You flatter me," he said.

"Not at all," Floyd assured him. "I know what I'm talking about. I'm an expert, you know."

"I'm exceptional," Ashes agreed. "Which is why I will succeed where my predecessors have failed."

"Not going to happen," Floyd said, shaking his head. "It's too early in the game."

"How so?"

"Oh, you know," Floyd said vaguely. "Supervillains have only been around a few months. Hardly long enough for someone to win. If there's going to be a winner it won't be until later this year, at least."

"There are no such rules," Ashes sneered. "Come up with a better reason why I can't succeed."

"Oh let's see," Floyd pretended to think. "Fire weakens you?"

Ashes bristled. "The fire makes me stronger!" he exclaimed.

"And that's why you look exhausted?" Floyd taunted. "You have to stop burning once you've exhausted yourself. What happens if you didn't? Would you die? Would you get stronger?"

Ashes smiled. "Nothing can kill me," he said.

"Don't be too sure of that," Floyd said. "I'm very good at what I do. Expert, remember?"

Ashes held up his hand and flames shot out in a beam towards Floyd. The alien yelped and rolled out of the way.

"Hold on!" he said, holding up both hands in a gesture of peace. "I'm not done talking yet!"

Ashes laughed. "You're afraid," he taunted.

"Yes, I am," Floyd said. "In a very healthy 'I don't want to die' sort of way."

"You don't want the Great Blaze to come," Ashes said. "But I will teach you not to be afraid."

"I'll keep my fear, thank you very much," Floyd said. "Tell me more about this Great Blaze. What kind of game are you playing?"

"I want to burn the entire Earth," Ashes said. "Everything will be consumed in beautiful, glorious fire."

"Really," Floyd said sarcastically, stepping towards him again. "And how long will that take? Six hundred years?"

"Every day I get stronger," Ashes whispered, beckoning him closer. "Every day I will burn longer and hotter and brighter. Every day brings me closer to what you dread."

"Really?" Floyd said, cautiously approaching. "What *I* dread? What could that possibly be?"

The answer made his blood run cold.

"The Second Great Fire of London," the human torch said, smiling at the thought. "The blaze that will level the city you protect at such great personal cost."

Unexpectedly he reached out and caught Floyd's wrist. Floyd bit his tongue, but couldn't wipe the pain from his eyes. Ashes smiled as smoke began to rise from under his fingers. Floyd wrenched free and retreated to the other side of the room.

Ashes's coarse laughter filled the room. Floyd decided he was done talking.

In the corner of the room was a pile of rubble. He stepped in front of it, reaching behind him for a long, heavy pipe.

"You betray yourself," Ashes said. "You are weak, and cannot bear to be near my greatness."

"Now you think you're some kind of god?" Floyd sighed. "Come on. You villains are all the same. I will rule the world, blah blah. I will destroy you all, blah blah. You are weak, etc ad nauseum. Would it kill you to be a little bit original?"

"Your words are big," Ashes said. "But you are powerless against me."

"Is that so?" Floyd said. "Then what's that over there?"

Predictably, Ashes turned his head. Floyd took the opportunity and hit him with a very heavy pipe.

Ashes burst into flame.

Floyd ran.

He ran faster than he'd ever run before, but the fire was faster still. He tripped and stumbled and it caught up with him. A flight of stairs gave way and he fell, but the fire came after and caught him. He couldn't see. He couldn't breathe. And he was burning.

The nanobots in his blood stream could knit together bone and flesh, they could stop bleeding and keep his brain supplied with oxygen, but they couldn't reassemble him out of a heap of ash. If he died here, he would never come back.

The building was bigger than he remembered, or maybe he was lost and running in circles. He realised he would never make it out, and that's when something hit him. The force of it threw him backwards and he gasped for breath in the sudden cold. Vaguely he realised that he was being rescued.

STRENGTH

Floyd didn't want to wake up. The part of his mind that still responded to who-knew-how-many months of training and conditioning acknowledged the fact that he wasn't done regenerating and insisted he stay asleep. But the rest of him, which had been living with humans for over two years, realised that the proper thing to do was rarely the best option and that whatever was prompting him to get up was probably right. Floyd gave in and opened his eyes.

The first thing he noticed was the complete absence of Sergeant Adams standing over him. Puzzled, he sat up, wincing with every move. His burns had healed nicely during the night but they still hurt as badly as ever.

He found his clothes in a surprisingly tidy pile on a chair beside his bed with a note pinned to the top. It was an address.

He stumbled through the motions of getting washed and dressed and forced his sleepy brain to focus on getting to where he was going.

Predictably, the location was very smoky.

"Oh good, you're here," Sergeant Adams said, and then frowned. "You put your shirt on backwards."

"Oh shut up," Floyd said. "What's going on?"

"It's bad," Adams said.

"What's going on?" Floyd repeated.

"It's really bad," Adams said. "Several hundred years ago there was a fire—"

"I know, all right?" Floyd interrupted. "We're standing near Pudding Lane, for Pete's sake. I know my history."

"Sorry," Adams said meekly.

"It's the Second Great Fire of London," Floyd admitted. "He told me and I looked it up before I came over."

"Then I'm not sorry," Adams said calmly. "Did he tell you anything else useful?"

"I think he did," Floyd said, running his fingers through his hair. "I just don't remember exactly."

"Now would be a good time to come up with something useful," Adams said. "Seeing as he's going to burn down the whole city."

"I doubt he can," Floyd said. "He's not strong enough yet. He can only burn a certain amount of time and then he has to regenerate..."

"And you can't kill him?"

"He seems to be invulnerable," Floyd said.

"Water doesn't have any affect," Adams pointed out. "So what can hurt him? Everyone has a weakness right?"

"Well," Floyd hesitated. "This might sound crazy."

Adams glared.

"Right," Floyd said hastily. "I don't think he cares much for fire."

"What?" Adams said incredulously.

"I think it's the only thing that can hurt him," Floyd said eagerly, warming up to the topic. "It's unusual, I know, but it also fits with the rules. His greatest strength is also his greatest weakness. Fire is what gives him his power and it's also the only thing that can destroy him."

"But he's on fire right now," Adams pointed out. "And he seems to be getting stronger."

"But he has to regenerate," Floyd said. "What happens if we don't let him?"

"What do you mean?"

"When he's attacked he reacts by turning to flame," Floyd pointed out. "If we keep forcing him to burn I think, maybe, it will burn him out."

"And if it doesn't?" Adams argued. "If he burns down the city and we hasten it along?"

"If it doesn't work the city will burn sooner or later," Floyd said tersely. "It might as well be sooner."

"Fire Chief Riley asked to see you as soon as you showed up," Adams said. "You'd better go tell him this insane plan of yours."

"I will," Floyd said. "Just point me in the right direction."

....

"You look surprisingly well," Riley said in greeting.

"It's one of the more useful side-effects of being an alien from outer space," Floyd said seriously. "How many people are going to die from this latest stunt?"

"Not very many," Riley reassured him. "He seems to be going for style rather than casualties."

Floyd swore. "I wish he would pick a pattern and stick to it," he said bitterly. "You're sure you were able to get people out in time?"

"Do you know how many people died in the first great fire of London?" Riley asked. "Six. Believe me, we've got it under control. Now do you have a way to stop this guy?"

"His strength has a limit," Floyd explained. "He burns until he's exhausted and then he has to rest and recover before he can burn again."

"So?"

"So we push him past that limit," Floyd said. "We don't let him rest. We push him until he can't go any further and then we shove him over the edge and turn him into a pile of ash."

Riley's brow furrowed in thought. "Are you sure that will work?" he asked.

"No," Floyd snapped. "But it's our best chance."

"Are you sure?" Riley asked insistently.

Floyd stared up at him and considered. "I'm sure," he said finally. "Everyone has a weakness, and his is fire."

"All right," Riley said, making a decision. "How do we keep this fire going?"

"Antagonise him," Floyd said. "Keep watering him, that's a good start. If it goes out send someone in to hit him or shoot him or be otherwise threatening. I can keep up with it for the most part, but you'll need your men to watch it. Make sure no one gets hurt."

"Stay here," Riley said. "I want to be able to find you if I need you."

60

Floyd looked around and found a seat. "Don't worry," he assured him. "I don't exactly feel like getting singed again."

....

The day went by slowly. Around noon Adams came over with sandwiches and they ate and watched the black cloud growing in the sky.

"How are you holding up?" Adams asked.

"Oh," Floyd shrugged. "I'm wishing I was safe at home and that I'd never heard of Earth or supervillains."

"Have you made any progress on your story?"

Floyd stared blankly. "What story?"

"The one about superheroes you're supposed to be writing."

"I told you I'm not writing that."

"I saw some of your attempts when I came by your house," Adams continued unperturbed. "They were very impressive. Government conspiracies, mysterious sightings..."

"I said I'm not writing it," Floyd said tersely.

"I think you should," Adams said. "It's just the sort to nonsense that the readers of your paper have come to expect."

"Are you making fun of me?" Floyd said in astonishment. "I'm sitting here trying to save the world and you brought me sandwiches so that you could ridicule my job?"

"It's not your job," Adams pointed out. "This is your job."

"No," Floyd argued. "This isn't a job—this is my life."

"I think you should write the story," Adams said bluntly.

"I said I'm not going to," Floyd replied. "Heroes don't exist."

"I think you should write it," Adams repeated. "Because heroes *do* exist."

"Not you, too," Floyd said in exasperation.

"Listen, Floyd," Adams said firmly. "Just because you've had a terrible life doesn't mean that there isn't any hope in the world. There are people who risk their lives selflessly for others every day and you can't live in denial of that fact."

"Heroes don't exist," Floyd snapped.

"Listen to yourself," Adams snapped back. "You sound like the Grinch Who Stole Christmas."

"The who that stole what?"

"People deserve hope," Adams continued, ignoring him, "and you have the power to give that to them."

"I thought you hated my job," Floyd muttered, standing up and brushing the crumbs off his trousers.

"What I hate is watching you lose hope," Adams said. Floyd looked back at him in surprise.

"You can't keep doing this."

"Doing what?" Floyd snapped. "Saving the world?"

"Walking around like this is some kind of curse—" Adams countered.

"It is a curse," Floyd interrupted.

"And that things will never get better," Adams finished smoothly. "You may not believe in heroes, Floyd, but without them we would be less than human."

"Forgive me," Floyd said sarcastically, "for not being the same as you."

"I didn't mean that," Adams said instantly, also standing.

"Yes, you did," Floyd said. "That's what all this comes down to—human beliefs, human needs human hopes; but *I'm not human*. And I never will be. I'll always be the outsider; the black cloud raining on everyone's parade. So just leave me alone and let me be miserable and hopeless and kill supervillains and work a crummy job because I can't get one anywhere else!"

"Excuse me," a fireman interrupted them. "I'm looking for Floyd."

"I'm Floyd," Floyd said. "Is something wrong?"

"It's the supervillain," the fireman said. "He wants to talk to you."

DETERMINATION

"Hello, Floyd," Ashes said, smiling. His eyes were dancing and glowing and when he gestured sparks flew from his fingertips. "I'm surprised to see you alive."

"Same here," Floyd said cautiously.

"I've never seen anyone survive being burned alive before."

"I've never seen anyone survive having their skull smashed in."

"I've never seen a fire damaged by a heavy pipe."

Floyd sighed. "What do you want?" he asked.

"I want to see you run," Ashes said, smiling again. "I want to see your eyes filled with fear and desperation. The end of the world is coming, Floyd. I am getting stronger. You cannot stop me, but I want to see you try."

He held out his hand and a flame sprang up out of his palm. Floyd took a step backwards.

"I've developed a distaste for hot situations," he said.

Ashes laughed. "You're afraid," he said triumphantly.

"I've got a healthy respect for pain and death," Floyd acknowledged.

"Come on," Ashes taunted. "The greatest hero in the world and you don't even want a rematch?"

"No," Floyd said. "I don't. The one thing you villains never seem to get is that I don't like confrontation. I don't like to beat you up with my bare hands. I don't like getting nearly killed, burned to death, thrown off buildings, decapitated, tortured, or any of things you seem to think I ought to enjoy."

"And yet you still try to defeat us."

"I do defeat you," Floyd asserted. "But I do it by sneaking up behind when you're not looking and hitting you on the head with a pipe. Much safer and more satisfactory all around."

"Except for when your villain turns to flame," Ashes pointed out.

"Well, yes," Floyd agreed. "That was a bit of a setback."

"A face to face confrontation is much more glorious," Ashes added. "Look at us now, conversing like great men from history!"

"Look," Floyd said impatiently. "There are a lot of you guys, and only one of me. I have to be as effective and efficient as possible. I don't have time for all these theatrics."

"Theatrics?" Ashes turned his hand over, as the whole thing became engulfed in flame. "Do you know what it's like to burn, Floyd?"

"Yes," Floyd said uneasily. "Thanks to you, I do."

"It's marvellous," Ashes continued, as though he hadn't heard him. "It's freedom and power. The heat and the motion... it consumes you and leaves you empty and longing for more, always, always more. And I will have it. One day, I will have it all. I will burn over the entire earth, and my glory will rival that of the sun."

"You're insane," Floyd said.

"You're afraid," Ashes countered.

"If you weren't a supervillain you'd be afraid too," Floyd argued.

"I can set you free," Ashes whispered. He took a step forward, more of his body turning to flame.

"No thank you," Floyd said, retreating hastily. "Some other time maybe."

Ashes laughed wildly. "There won't be any other time," he said. "The time is now. We will all burn together."

"What do you want?" Floyd snapped, losing patience. "You didn't stop your glorious destruction of the city of London to come argue with me—did you?"

"Isn't this what you want?" Ashes said. "Don't you long to see this city burn?"

"No," Floyd said decisively. "What gave you that idea?"

Ashes smiled again. "Why have your firemen ceased their attempts to stop me, and instead press me to burn longer and hotter than ever before?"

"You know what?" Floyd said, retreating a few more steps. "You're creepy. I don't like you. And I think we're done talking."

Ashes moved quickly, too quickly. He turned to liquid fire along the ground and reformed next to Floyd. Floyd could feel the heat emanating off of him, reawakening the burning feeling in his newly healed skin.

"I know that you're clever," Ashes hissed. "You're not going anywhere until you tell me where this sudden zeal for fire comes from."

Floyd stared uneasily. "I wrote a blog post about this," he said. "Feel free to look it up."

He turned and walked away but a fiery tendril lashed out and caught him around the waist.

Floyd screamed.

"Tell me," Ashes whispered into his ear, his breath hot on his face, his hands burning ice where they gripped his shoulders.

"Your greatest strength," Floyd hissed, "is your greatest weakness."

"What does that mean?" Ashes demanded.

Floyd wrenched out of his grasp and tumbled to the ground, gasping for breath.

"Figure it out!" he shouted. "If you're really so strong and so powerful you shouldn't need to ask me for help interpreting your own superpowers!"

Someone shouted in the distance, interupting. Ashes looked up and snarled at the distraction. In that brief moment of reprieve Floyd knew he was going to burn, and realised exactly how afraid he was.

There was a cold shower of water from high pressured hoses. There were shouted instructions and people coming towards him to drag him out of the way. Ashes roared into a column of flame that shot towards the sky. There was noise and confusion and then Adams was beside him, shaking him, and repeating something over and over again.

"Are you all right?" he was saying. "Are you all right?"

"I'm fine," Floyd said, brushing him away. "Why does everyone always say that?"

"There's been a situation," Adams said. "They need you over at the palace."

"The palace?" Floyd said incredulously. "What kind of a joke is that?"

"I'm serious," Adams said. "Apparently Doctor Sinister is demanding that you face him."

"Doctor Sinister?" Floyd coughed and looked back at the towering pillar of flame. "I don't have time for him right now."

"It's not a choice, Floyd."

"You're joking, right? Please tell me you're joking."

"They're sending a helicopter."

Floyd stared in dismay.

. . . .

The lawn in front of Buckingham Palace was covered with emergency personnel, police, and reporters. The police were doing their best to keep the spectators out, but they crowded as close as they could. The helicopter landed and Floyd looked around and sighed.

"Are you Jeffry Lewis Floyd?" an official-looking man in black demanded.

"That's me," Floyd said. "And I'll have you know I was in the middle of important business when you decided to abduct me."

"Listen closely," the agent snapped. "I don't know who you are or what your connection with that madman is, but he's threatening to blow London to oblivion unless you speak with him."

"That madman is, I take it, Doctor Sinister?" Floyd queried.

"That's what he calls himself, yes."

"And how does he plan on demolishing the city?"

"He says he has an antimatter bomb."

Floyd laughed in incredulity.

"This is very serious," the agent snapped.

"I'm sure it is," Floyd said. "And that's why you're all turned out over an anti—"

He couldn't finish his sentence for hilarity.

"Floyd," Adams snapped. "Get a grip."

"What are you doing here, Sergeant?" the official demanded.

Adams stiffened to attention.

"Hey," Floyd intervened. "He's with me. We were working together on a case."

"And you are who, exactly?" the agent demanded.

Floyd shrugged. "I'm a reporter," he said. "But no one seems to believe that any more."

The agent gave up on responding to that.

"Doctor Sinister is a madman," he said. "And he's extremely dangerous. We don't know what he wants with you—"

He broke off in confusion as Floyd started laughing again.

"What is so funny?" he demanded.

"Antimatter bombs," Floyd chuckled. "I can't believe you fell for that. Antimatter..."

The agent looked at Adams. Adams shrugged.

"They don't exist," Floyd explained, grinning with delight. "There is no such thing. He's bluffing."

"Bluffing?" the agent said, raising his eyebrows.

"Bluffing," Floyd said confidently. "You can go arrest him now."

"I don't think we can take that risk," the agent said uncertainly.

"I think you can," Floyd said. "Can I go now?"

"No," Adams and the agent both said at once.

"Seriously?" Floyd said. "Do I have to do everything myself?"

"It could be dangerous," the agent repeated stiffly.

"Really," Floyd said sarcastically. "Dangerous. I guess I do have to do everything myself. Point me at the nearest staircase, please."

"I'll show you the way," the agent said.

"Do you want to get us all killed?" Floyd snapped, suddenly all business. "I said *point* the way. I'm going up alone."

"But you said he was bluffing," the agent said, thrown off guard.

"And you said we couldn't take that chance," Floyd retorted. "So are you willing to risk it or not?"

"Who *are* you?" the agent demanded.

"I'm not at liberty to discuss that," Floyd said, narrowing his eyes

The agent gave him directions without another comment, and Floyd set off at a run

"Stairs," he grumbled to no one in particular as he began to climb. "Everyone acts like they're so simple. Just climb that flight of stairs until you run into the next irritation on your schedule..."

He came out onto the roof and glared into the setting sun. Doctor Sinister turned in a particular dramatic manner and smiled.

"Floyd," he said. "How good of you to come."

"Give me the bomb," Floyd said without preamble, striding across the roof towards him.

"What?" Doctor Sinister said, feigning ignorance. "What bomb?"

"The antimatter bomb," Floyd said. "Give it here. Now."

Doctor Sinister laughed. "They don't exist."

"Yeah, I know that," Floyd said. "Now give it to me."

"Why should I do that?

"Because if you don't," Floyd said conversationally, "I will break your neck."

Doctor Sinister instantly produced a shiny red bauble

"All right," Floyd said, sticking his hands in his pockets. "What do you want?"

"I want," Doctor Sinister said, spreading his hands, "what I have always wanted. To defeat you, my nemesis, here, with the whole world watching us."

"I am not your nemesis," Floyd said crossly, "the whole world is not watching us, and stop waving that thing around."

"Thing?" Doctor Sinister held up the object in question. "This is most devastating device ever created in man's history."

Floyd folded his arms. Doctor Sinister looked flustered for a moment and then continued

"This, my dear fellow, is an antimatter bomb. If it is set off it will create a hole in the universe roughly the same size as the city. No messy explosions just—whup! And you're gone."

"And you too," Floyd pointed out.

"I didn't actually intend on using it," Doctor Sinister said. "It was simply a ploy to get you to come."

"That's exactly what it was," Floyd said crossly. "I'll have you know I was in the middle of a very important conference when I heard about your childish stunts."

"Childish?" Doctor Sinister said, offended. "Childish? I am standing upon the most important building in London and you say that I am being childish? What child could possibly manage to do all that I've done?"

"All you've managed to do so far is to ruin my day!" Floyd said. "Now will you tell me what you want so I can get back to work on real issues?"

"What kind of *real* issues could you possibly have that are more important than dealing with me?" Doctor Sinister roared. "You insult me!"

"Yes, I do. Now can I go please?"

"Not until you defeat... me"

Floyd stuck his hands in his pockets. "I would really rather not," he said.

Doctor Sinister stuck his face close to Floyd's.

"You will battle with me," he threatened, "Or I will use my 'little toy' to destroy your city."

"Not going to happen," Floyd said.

"Why not?" Doctor Sinister demanded.

"Because there's no such thing," Floyd stated. "Your flashy bauble is as harmless as your haircut."

Instinctively Doctor Sinister reached up a hand to touch his head. "What's wrong with my haircut?" he demanded.

"Give me the bomb," Floyd said, holding out his hand and waggling his fingers.

Doctor Sinister held the bomb over his head, his finger posed on the trigger.

Floyd sighed. "Do I have to?" he whined.

"You have to," Doctor Sinister asserted.

"Fine," Floyd said. "A duel, to the death, on top of Buckingham Palace, between the world's most terrible villain—Doctor Sinister, and the world's only alien photojournalist, Jeffry Lewis Floyd."

Doctor Sinister lowered his hands and smiled. "Exactly," he said.

"Give me that," Floyd said, and snatched the bomb away.

He had to jump to reach it, but Doctor Sinister was caught off guard and didn't react in time. Floyd tossed it over the edge and far below on the palace lawn it caused several dozen agents of various kinds to leap into a panicked search for the object, afraid that at any moment it would go off and swallow them all.

Ironically Adams found it. He held it up in his hand—a shiny, red, child's ball.

"I told you it was a bluff," Floyd said, coming up behind him. "Can we go now?"

"But you said it was dangerous!" the agent protested.

"You said it was dangerous," Floyd corrected. "I was just parroting you."

Adams looked around. "Where's Doctor Sinister?" he asked.

"He's dead," Floyd said tersely.

"Dead?" Adams and the agent in black queried at once.

"I broke his neck," Floyd said. "I'm sick and tired of him getting in my way. Now, if you don't mind, I've got to make sure the entire city doesn't burn down tonight."

SACRIFICE

Heroism (n.)
1. exhibiting or marked by courage
2. daring or supremely noble or self-sacrificing

The fire lit up the night with an orange glow that could be seen for miles.

"You're sure you don't want to go home?" Adams asked.

"Shut up," Floyd snapped, uncharacteristically harsh.

"You don't have to be here," Adams pressed. "You can go home and I'll call if anything changes."

"And if I get here too late?" Floyd asked sharply. "What happens then?"

Adams didn't answer.

"Welcome back," Riley said wearily, looking up as they approached.

"How is the fire?" Floyd asked shortly.

"It's getting weaker," Riley said. "Just like you said."

"And smaller?" Floyd asked hopefully.

The fire chief shoved some maps at him. "Not by much," he said.

"We just have to wait," Floyd said. "Sooner or later he has to burn out."

"And then?" Riley asked. "What if he's still alive as a human?"

"I'll burn him alive," Floyd said grimly. "Keep me posted; I'm going to go grab a front-row seat."

He stalked off without another word. Adams hesitated, and then followed him.

"Floyd!" he called after him.

"Don't you have any traffic to direct?" Floyd asked irritably.

"I'm off duty," Adams said.

"Well what do you want?"

"I want to know why you're doing this," Adams said.

"Because," Floyd said with exaggerated patience. "Because if I fall asleep I won't be able to wake back up."

"Not that," Adams said. "This. Everything. Why are you doing it?"

"What do you mean?"

"You could just go home and sleep," Adams said. "If Ashes wins then you could just skip town. Why do you bother fighting the supervillains when you know more will just rise up in their place?"

"It's my job," Floyd said uneasily.

"No, it's not," Adams countered swiftly. "It's your curse. But it's not like your alien overlords are watching to make sure you do what they sent you for. You can walk away."

"And if the supervillains destroy Earth?" Floyd snorted. "Then where does that leave me?"

"Do you really think you're making a difference?" Adams taunted. "A villain here, a mastermind there? How does the rest of the world cope without you if you're that important?"

Floyd didn't answer.

"You're not human," Adams continued in a tone of disdain, throwing his own words back at him. "This isn't your world; isn't your fight. Why do you care what happens? Why don't you just keep running and live a happy life for as long as you can before the inevitable end?"

"Someone has to," Floyd muttered.

"Someone else can," Adams snapped. "Why you?"

"No one else can!" Floyd said in frustration. "That's why I was sent here!"

"So is that the reason you do it?" Adams said. "You do it because 'no one else can'? You'd better come up with a better reason than that, or I'm going to lose any interest I had in helping you."

"What?" Floyd's anger suddenly turned to panic. "What do you mean?"

"If you're only doing this because you have to," Adams said, "Then one day you're going to get tired of it and walk away. And if that's the case I think I'd be better off helping someone who plans to stick with the job."

"Who?" Floyd said. "I told you, there is no one."

"I'll find someone," Adams said grimly. "There are always heroes."

Floyd opened his mouth to protest and shut it again.

"I'm not a hero," he said finally. He spoke quietly, all will to fight gone out of him.

"Why are you doing this?" Adams repeated forcefully.

"Heroes get killed!" Floyd protested. "And people are always expecting them to... be heroic."

"Why are you doing this?" Adams asked.

Floyd struggled to come up with an answer.

Adams folded his arms and waited.

With a sudden woosh the fire went out, and Floyd's attention was diverted.

He turned and ran back towards the fire engines, and Adams followed without question.

"Is it really out?" he asked Riley, panicking.

"Completely," the fire chief assured him.

"Can you show me roughly the centre of the area?" Floyd asked.

"What are you going to do?" Adams asked.

Riley shoved a map at him and pointed to a red dot.

"I need kerosene," Floyd said. "Or petrol. Anything that will burn, really. And any kind of weapon would be nice. Even something large, heavy, and blunt."

"Will this work?" one of the firemen handed him a long axe.

"That's great," Floyd said.

"What are you going to do?" Adams repeated.

"I told you earlier," Floyd said. "I'm going to burn him alive."

"That could be dangerous," Riley said.

"I'll take the chance," Floyd said tersely. "Someone has to."

Someone handed him a pile of fire fighting gear and he put it on. Adams watched uneasily.

"Why are you doing this?" he asked.

"I'm not a hero," Floyd said tersely, putting on the heavy fire coat. It reached nearly to his knees but he didn't notice. "Because being a hero takes courage," he continued. "And that's something I don't have. Putting the right tools into a person's hands doesn't make them a hero. Heroes are brave. They're willing to die for someone else and I—I can't die."

He straightened up and met Adams' eyes. "I can walk into a stream of bullets because I know I'll get up and walk away from it," he explained. "It will hurt a whole lot, but it won't kill me. I don't have to risk my life, because I haven't got a life to risk. And those who do...

"It takes courage," he said vehemently. "And it takes a whole lot of stupidity. And I could never do it—what these firemen do. What the special agents at the palace do. If I didn't have these bots in my system I would turn and run at the first sight of danger."

He took a deep breath and went on. "They're the heroes," he said. "Give them their due, and stop trying to praise me."

....

Ashes hadn't even tried to stand. He lay on the ground, coughing and broken. His skin was pale grey, and he was a shrivelled weakened version of his former self. His clothes were torn and filthy, barely covering him. He was a man absolutely defeated, with no hope of survival. But when he saw Floyd coming, he laughed.

"Hello, Ashes," Floyd said quietly.

"One day I will burn over the entire earth, and my glory will rival that of the sun," Ashes rasped. His voice was hoarse and faint. Speaking brought on another coughing fit. He raised himself to his elbows, and Floyd waited patiently until he had finished hacking.

"This ends now," he said, when he had the villain's attention. "It's over."

"You can't stop me," Ashes said. "I will burn."

The one thing about him that had not changed was the ingratiating grin that made Floyd want to squirm. This time he managed to control himself.

"Yes," he agreed. "We are going to burn. Just not in the way you think."

"You can't destroy... fire," Ashes said weakly.

"You've destroyed yourself," Floyd said. "You couldn't start a fire now if your life depended on it. You can't even stand on your own. In fact, if I simply walked away and left you it's entirely possible that you'd die of starvation before you recovered your strength."

"But you won't do that," Ashes said, and smiled again.

"No," Floyd said. "I won't."

"Because you can't—can't walk away and... leave a man to die."

"Yes, I can," Floyd said harshly. "I've done it before. Don't make any mistake, Ashes. You're not coming out of this alive."

"You're not even going to... give me a chance? What kind of a hero are you?"

"You had your chance the day I met you," Floyd said, ignoring the second question. "You chose to kill when you could have chosen not to, and I'm not in the habit of handing out lives like a parole officer giving his prisoners spare change."

"You're going to kill me? In cold blood?"

"No," Floyd smiled. "You're going to burn."

"I... can't..."

Ashes held out his hand, and focused. His fingers trembled with the effort but not a single spark flicked from his fingers. The effort exhausted him and he fell back on the black-scorched ground.

"You can't—you can't kill me," Ashes protested, reality sinking in. "It's unethical. It's—merciless."

"What you've done is unethical," Floyd retorted. "What you've done is merciless."

"I'm the villain," Ashes smiled. "You're not. You have behave according to civilisation's rules."

"Where do people get these preconceived notions about what I can and cannot do?" Floyd demanded. "Let me tell you something, you miserable pile of firewood. You're going to die, right here, right now, and I am going to kill you, heartlessly, and mercilessly. I do not fit into your little box labelled 'heroism,' and I don't intend to try. I was sent to keep this world safe, not to live up to some kind of ideal you've all invented of what my job should look like. Now, if you don't mind, I'd like to get on with my work."

He unbuckled his belt and dropped it to the ground. There were two canteens of kerosene which he proceeded to dump over Ashes and the surrounding area. The villain watched him, half-curious and half-mocking. When he was finished he crouched down next to Ashes, a lighter in his hands.

"This is it," he said softly. "Say your prayers—because this is the end for you."

"I don't understand," Ashes mumbled, beginning to lose his confidence. "What are you doing?"

"Guess," Floyd said, a smile of his own spreading across his face. The lighter produced a sudden flame and the kerosene started on fire.

Floyd ran.

Behind him the tiny point of fire he'd started ran across the ground, eagerly devouring whatever it came into contact with, springing into a bright wall of flame, leaping towards the sky, dancing, crackling, showering sparks. It burned the clothes off of Ashes's back first, and then bit into his skin. Floyd heard the villain's harsh, startled cry of pain and ran faster, but something reached out and tripped him.

Panicking, he scrambled to his knees and tried to stand, but it wrapped itself around him, and pulled him back. The tendrils burned wherever they came into contact, and he recognised it as Ashes's touch. He opened his mouth to scream but heat rushed into his lungs and he fell back into its fiery embrace.

The fire crept into Ashes. It filled his lungs and his thoughts. He felt himself fraying apart, giving away to it, but he didn't let go of his prisoner. He screamed with agony, but he heard the alien screaming too and it gave him satisfaction somehow. His last thoughts were that this was what it meant to really burn, and then he dissolved into oblivion.

10 HOPE

Floyd woke up.

This occurrence was important enough that he took a moment to observe it before moving on to other things like figuring out where he was, what had happened, and why he was in so much pain.

He opened his eyes and shut them against the burning light.

And then he remembered, and swore violently.

"Floyd?" a startled voice cut through his thoughts and the roar in his mind that brought back every second he'd been trapped in that fire.

He didn't want to face Adams, he didn't want to face anyone. He rolled over on his side and tried to pretend nothing was happening.

"Floyd, are you all right?" the voice came closer.

"Go away," he mumbled, but his voice caught on the dryness in his throat and he sat up coughing.

Someone put a glass of water in his hands and the coldness of it quenched some of the burning on his skin and in his mind. He drank it all and dropped the glass, blinking back the sudden tears that burned behind his eyelids.

"Thank you," he whispered.

"Are you feeling better?" Adams asked.

Floyd hesitated, and then nodded. "I'm alive," he commented.

"The firemen rescued you," Adams explained.

"Again? How many times does that make?"

"Three."

"Darn," Floyd said in amazement. "I should send them a card or something."

"That would probably be nice," Adams agreed.

Floyd tried opening his eyes again. The room swam out of focus and he closed them again.

"Ashes?" he asked. "Is he out rampaging and killing and burning again?"

"He's dead," Adams said.

"You saw a body?"

"There was no body," the policeman explained. "And believe me, we combed that area. The only thing left there was you. Ashes is gone."

"So it worked, then," Floyd said, daring to hope.

"You've been out for days," Adams said. "If he were still alive I think we would have heard from him."

Floyd winced at the reminder. "I think I've arrived at a conclusion," he said.

"What would that be?" Adams asked.

"I don't like fire."

"That's understandable," Adams said. Floyd opened his eyes again and took in the time of day,

86

the state of the room, and the fact that Adams was holding the glass he'd previously dropped.

"Is this going to happen every time?" he asked pitifully. "I'm going to meet some big baddie and he's going to nearly kill me?"

"I think you'll probably get better with practice," Adams said consolingly.

Floyd curled up on the bed and stared at the wall beyond Adams.

"I don't like getting killed," he admitted.

"No one does," Adams said.

"I don't like people dying."

Adams had nothing to say.

"I couldn't save them," Floyd said. "The people Ashes killed—I can't bring them back."

"Floyd..."

"And it will never stop," he continued, agitated. "Supervillains will keep killing people, and I'll keep killing supervillains, and then something will kill me and I'll wake up some morning and it will start all over again...

"And what's the point of it?" he asked forcefully. "What is the point of being a hero if you can't save people?"

"I... I don't know," Adams said slowly. "I just know that you can't quit trying because of it."

"But I can't keep doing this," Floyd protested. "I just... I want the killing to stop."

"It will," Adams tried to promise. "Someday—"

"No, it won't!" Floyd interrupted, sitting up again. "That's the point. Even when the supervillains are gone the evil won't be. It's all over the world, all over the galaxy, and there will always be people suffering somewhere, dying..."

"And you can make a difference," Adams snapped. "You can't stop it, you can't save everyone, but you can save some. You can help a few."

"But it doesn't matter in the long run," Floyd argued.

"That's not important," Adams said. "It matters to the people you help. It matters to the people who didn't die because you stopped Ashes before he got to them."

"It doesn't make a difference," Floyd said stubbornly.

"Yes, it does," Adams said. "I've been fighting evil for six years now; you've been at it for about two months. I know what makes a difference and what doesn't."

"But people will keep getting killed?" Floyd asked.

"Yes."

"And I'll keep waking up in pain?"

"Probably."

"Then what's the point?"

"The point is that I said there's a point," Adams said matter-of-factly. "And I have to go to work, so I don't have time to have the same conversation with you all day."

He stood up. "Have a nice day, Floyd," he said.

He paused in the doorway. "Oh," he added. "I suggest you work on getting your job back. Seeing as how supervillains don't pay you to kill them."

"Maybe I don't want my job back!" Floyd tried to protest, but Adams was gone.

Floyd sighed and looked around. Whatever he might say, Adams was right, and he should get to work.

Half an hour later the kitchen floor was once again littered with discarded pieces of paper, with headlines like "Do heroes exist?" and "What are heroes?" and "Why am I doing this anyway?"

He was interrupted by the unusual sound of a knock on the door.

He froze mid-sentence and stared at it, waiting for the sound to come again. It did.

Curious, he stood and walked towards it. No one ever knocked on his door. No one. Because no one ever bothered to come see him except for Adams, and Adams never bothered to knock.

He yanked it open suspiciously, unsure what he would find on the other side, and stared in astonishment at—

"Chief Riley?" he said, blinking. He almost didn't recognise the fire chief. Without the fire helmet, he could see that his hair was beginning to grey, and without the grime and soot, his eyes were less worried and more open and humorous.

"Floyd," the fire chief said. "Sergeant Adams told me you would be awake, so I thought I'd come back and see how you were doing."

Floyd stepped back and held open the door wordlessly.

The fire chief came in and Floyd closed the door, noticing for the first time the mess on his floor and his own state of attire.

"I'm afraid I wasn't expecting guests," he said uncertainly, but Riley shut him up with a wave of his hand.

"I came to see you," he stated. "Not your flat."

He shoved some dirty clothes out of the way and settled himself on the sofa as though he belonged there. Floyd sat back at the table and pulled his knees up to his chin anxiously.

"How are you?" Riley asked.

"Fine," Floyd said shortly.

Riley raised his eyebrows.

"Thank you for saving my life," Floyd blurted out. "Three times," he added.

"Oh that," Riley brushed it aside. "That was an honour."

"Honour?" Floyd said in astonishment. "I could have got everyone there killed."

"But you didn't," Riley said. "You risked your own life to save that of other people. Now, me and the other firemen, we're trained to do that. What's your excuse?"

"I..." Floyd tried to answer and trailed off. "I'm trained too," he said finally.

"Not to fight fires," Riley stated.

"Well, no..."

"What then?"

"To kill supervillains," Floyd explained.

"You're doing a very good job," the fire chief said.

Floyd looked up in surprise. "I am?" he asked.

"You took out two in one day," Riley said. "That's impressive."

"It is?" Floyd repeated. "I mean, I do that all the time. Kill supervillains, I mean."

"A team of experts couldn't do what I've seen you do," Riley said frankly. "You're smart, you're quick to think up solutions, and you're not afraid to risk your life to save others."

"You don't understand," Floyd said, shaking his head. "I can risk my life because I know I won't die. I..." he gestured helplessly, trying to explain.

"Some kind of bioengineering," the fire chief said. "Sergeant Adams mumbled something vague about that. Listen, it doesn't matter. How do you know if that technology is going to hold up the next time?"

"I—I don't," Floyd stammered.

"And how do you know that one of those villains won't just cut off your head?"

Floyd shrugged.

"Stop selling yourself short," the fire chief said. "What you did out there was amazing, and I'm *proud* to have had a chance to work beside you."

He stood up and held out his right hand. Floyd stared up at him.

"Do you mean that?" he asked, disbelieving.

"I do," Riley repeated, still holding out his hand. Hesitantly, Floyd unfolded himself from his chair and accepted the handshake.

"Get some rest," Riley said, clapping him on the shoulder. "This city needs you back up and fighting."

He let himself out, because Floyd stood frozen in the middle of the room until long after he was gone.

....

The little bell on the door that led to the offices of the London Star tinkled merrily as Floyd walked through.

"I didn't expect to see you here again," Mary Margaret commented, looking up from her work.

"Is Mr. Hendrick in his office?" Floyd asked.

She raised both of her perfectly manicured eyebrows. "He's rather testy right now," she warned. "I'm not sure you want to go in there unless you—"

Floyd walked past her without listening, and entered the Editor's office without knocking.

"If that's not the proof go away," the editor said without raising his head. Floyd threw the papers in his hand on the desk in front of him.

"What the—" he looked up angrily, and broke off when he saw Floyd. "What are you doing here?" he demanded. "I thought you resigned on moral grounds or something."

"I'm back now," Floyd said confidently. "You said not to come back without a superhero story, and I have one."

Mr. Hendrick glanced down at the printed sheet. "Why the world doesn't need superheroes," he read aloud.

"Don't expect that kind of sensationalist junk from me every week," Floyd said warningly. "I've got better things to do with my life."

"Sensationalist?" the editor spluttered. "What kind of paper do you think this is?"

"If you don't like it, I'll take it to the Times," Floyd added. "See you next Monday."

"Get back here!" the Editor roared. "We aren't done talking! You can't just walk out on me you—you—"

"I'm sorry," Floyd said, smiling as he opened the office door. "But I've got a world to save."

And the editor stared speechlessly as he left, closing the door as he went out.

SNEAK PEEK

Don't miss
Supervillain of the Day: Book 3
"Inspector Floyd"
Coming May 3rd, 2013!

Inspector McCormick greeted them enthusiastically. "Ah, Adams! Come in. Floyd, thank you for coming. Have a seat."

Floyd sat. Adams stood at the door, watching him. McCormick perched on the edge of his desk and handed photographs to Floyd.

"We've had four murders now," he said. "Two in my district, two over on the east side. They're all killed the same way," he passed Floyd another picture,"But the times of death are too similar. They can't all be committed by the same person."

"So you think you're looking for someone with super speed?" Floyd caught on quickly.

"Either that or multiple people working for the same leader," McCormick agreed. "That was your friend's idea actually, which is why I asked you to come down here."

Floyd looked through the rest of the pictures.

"Not super speed," he said. "Not super strength either. In fact, I'd say whoever did this would have to be very much human."

"Why?" McCormick asked. Floyd looked up in surprise.

"The force of the blow," he said, as if it were obvious. "If the killer had superpowers the knife would have gone clean through."

"So what about a villain with some other kind of power?" McCormick asked. "Freezing his victim or... or appearing as an illusion or something?"

"It wasn't a villain," Floyd said, shaking his head. "There's no anger or violence in these killings."

"Killings are the definition of anger and violence!" Adams exclaimed.

"Yes," Floyd agreed. "But these bodies are intact, left in the street, with the knife still in them. This is a human crime."

McCormick scratched his head. "Walk me through it," he said.

Floyd sighed. "Okay," he said. "Villains are driven by hate, anger, greed, etc."

"So are people," Adams pointed out.

"Right," Floyd said, irritated, "But in villains these traits are amplified. So while a human might kill someone in a bout of anger, that's not enough for an angry villain. He's not going to kill - he's going to tear the body apart limb from limb."

"So maybe the villain wasn't angry?" Adams suggested.

Floyd shook his head. "You don't understand," he said. "Villains don't commit murders. Massacres, yes. They take prisoners, they torture them to death. They take hostages to prove a point, but they don't skulk around in the dead of the night killing random strangers. It's not their style. They're as proud as they are evil and they want everyone to know what they're doing and why they're doing it."

He stood up and brushed his hands together. "This man was killed by an ordinary human being like you or me. Well, not like me," he amended, "like you or Sergeant Adams here."

McCormick stood too. "So, what about the discrepancies in the times of death?" he asked. "If it was just one person how did he manage to kill all those people?"

"I don't know," Floyd said shortly. "That's your problem, not mine."

"Floyd," Adams said, catching his arm as he turned to leave.

"Look, I've got my own problems," Floyd snapped. "You deal with yours and I'll take care of mine."

"Haven't found the owner of those dampening fields yet?" McCormick said.

Floyd stopped in surprise. "Yes," he admitted, "among other things."

"Are you sure?" McCormick asked, looking him straight in the eye. "Are you absolutely positive that these murders are in no way connected to any supervillains?"

Floyd hesitated for a fraction of a second. "Yes," he lied. "I'm sure."

"Thank you for your time, Mr. Floyd," McCormick said, sticking out his hand.

Floyd shook it, confused by the inspector's appreciative attitude, and left the station.

Adams sat in the seat he'd vacated and sighed. "He's lying," he said bluntly. "He's just trying to get out of here as quickly as possible."

"I know," McCormick said, walking around the desk. "But he was very helpful. Go home and get some rest, Sergeant. If we need him again, we'll call you."

To report a supervillain
or learn more about the series,
visit:

<u>supervillainoftheday.com</u>

A NOTE ABOUT ENGLAND

Being an American writing about England is one of the most terrifying and exhilarating things I have ever done. I've done my best to be as accurate as possible when setting this series in London, but we're all human and can make mistakes. If you're an expert or a resident of England and you find an error in this narrative, be sure to let me know about it! I'll take the correction under consideration when writing future novels, and possibly even correct the error in the omnibus version.

Submit errors using the form provided on supervillainoftheday.com and you could earn yourself a copy of the ebook version of the next novel in the series!

ABOUT THE AUTHOR

Katie is a writer of many talents, constantly branching out into new fields and genres. She primarily writes novels and short stories in the science fiction and fantasy genres, along with an assortment of hilarious and sentimental poetry. When she's not writing she's acting, directing, singing, playing her Celtic harp or songwriting, often engaging in more than one at a time. She lives in the beautiful hills of Kentucky with her parents and eight siblings.

Visit her website at katielynndaniels.com

Or follow her on twitter @danielskatie